P9-BZC-995

The I'M NOT SCARED Book

Todd Parr

Megan Tingley Books

LITTLE, BROWN AND COMPANY

New York   Boston

Little, Brown and Company
Hachette Book Group
1290 Avenue of the Americas, New York, NY 10104
Visit us at lb-kids.com

Originally published in hardcover by Little, Brown and Company in August 2011
First Trade Paperback Edition: July 2017

Little, Brown and Company is a division of Hachette Book Group, Inc.
The Little, Brown name and logo are trademarks of Hachette Book Group, Inc.

The publisher is not responsible for websites (or their content) that are not owned by the publisher.

The Library of Congress has cataloged the hardcover edition as follows:
Parr, Todd.
The I'm not scared book / Todd Parr. — 1st ed.
p. cm.
Summary: Relates the things that can frighten children and how these fears may be overcome.
ISBN 978-0-316-08445-1
[1. Fear—Fiction.] I. Title. II. Title: I am not scared book.
PZ7.P2447Im 2011
[E]—dc22
2010019252

ISBN: 978-0-316-43198-9 (pbk.)

10 9 8 7 6 5 4 3 2 1

APS

PRINTED IN CHINA

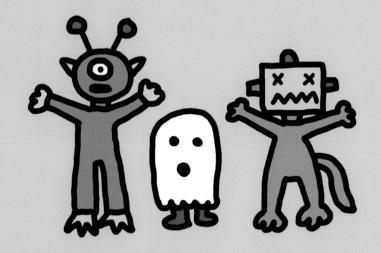

To Liza.
Love, Todd

I'm not scared if I have a night-light.

Sometimes I'm scared of dogs.

I'm not scared when they give me kisses.

Sometimes I'm scared to ride on an airplane.

I'm not scared when I see the world from above.

Sometimes I'm scared of monsters and ghosts.

I'm not scared when I see that they aren't real.

Sometimes I'm scared of what's under my bed.

I'm not scared once I clean
everything out and see all
my favorite toys.

Sometimes I'm scared when my family argues.

I'm not scared when we hug and say I'm sorry.

Sometimes I'm scared to go shopping for new underwear.

I'm not scared when I wear them on my head.

Sometimes I'm scared I will get lost in the grocery store.

I'm not scared when I stay close to Mommy.

Sometimes I'm scared on my first day of school.

'm not scared when I make new friends.

Sometimes I'm scared of thunder and lightning.

I'm not scared when I build a fort
with my best friend.

Sometimes I'm scared when I do something wrong.

I'm not scared when I help to fix it.

Sometimes I'm scared I will make a mistake.

I'm not scared when I know
I tried my best.

Sometimes I'm scared I'm not perfect.

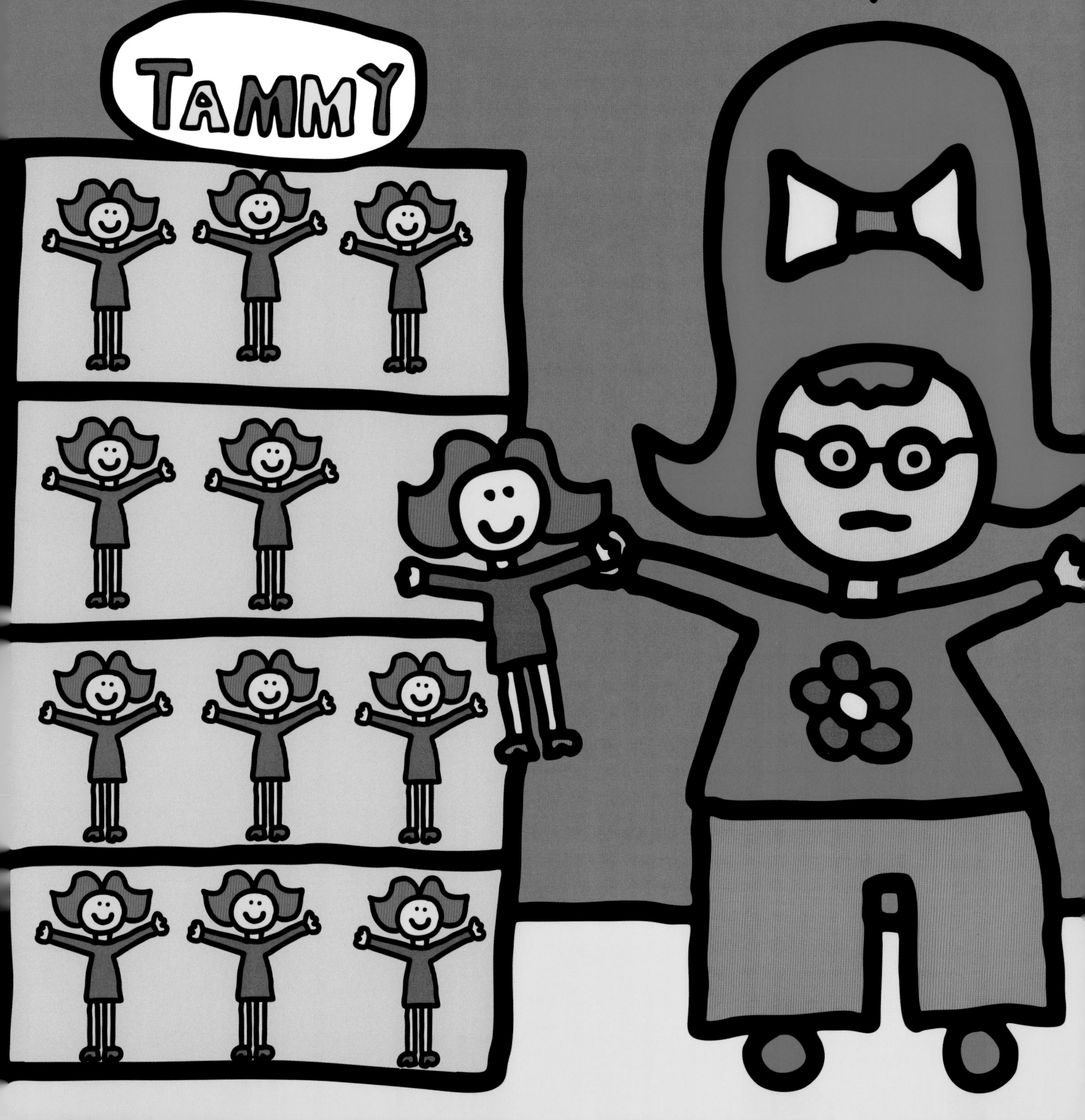

I'm not scared when I meet someone just like me.

Sometimes we are scared of things because we don't understand them.

When you are afraid, tell someone why and maybe you won't be scared anymore.

The End. Love, Todd

Jeff Fielding

Todd Parr has inspired and empowered children around the world with his bold images and positive messages. He is the bestselling author of more than forty books, including *Be Who You Are*, *The Family Book*, *The I Love You Book*, and *It's Okay to Be Different*. He lives in Berkeley, California.

Also by Todd Parr:

Be Who You Are	The Underwear Book
Teachers Rock!	Reading Makes You Feel Good
The Goodbye Book	The Feelings Book
It's Okay to Make Mistakes	The Feel Good Book
It's Okay to Be Different	The Peace Book
The Family Book	Otto Goes to School
The Mommy Book	Otto Goes to the Beach
The Daddy Book	Animals in Underwear ABC
The Grandma Book	Doggy Kisses 123
The Grandpa Book	

A complete list of Todd's books and more information
can be found at toddparr.com